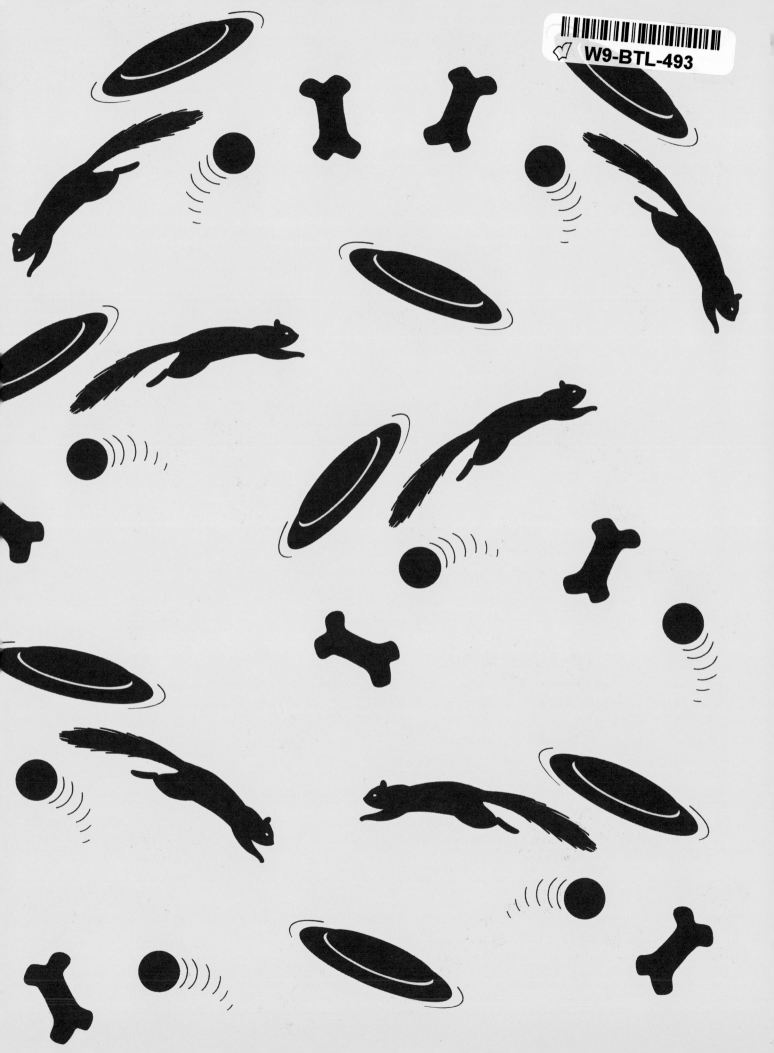

MURRAY'S
PRIVATE NIGHT OUT

A semi-true story

It started as a simple night out in Seattle, if any night in Seattle is simple. The occupants of 1251 on Capitol Hill were headed out to Murray's favorite Vietnamese restaurant, Madelyn at the wheel of her truck, Murray alert and comfortable at her side.

What had brought Murray to Seattle? The two-legged ones were not sure.

Murray had first met Madelyn as she toiled away in an English garden on Queen Anne Hill. "Madelyn the Gardener" was weeding, pruning and grooming the plants.

Murray just appeared out of nowhere, out of thin air, or so it seemed. Madelyn, a lover of canines, saw Murray and knew right away he was very special. He was a Corgi with a prized heritage from the British Isles.

Not knowing to whom or where he belonged,
she felt it was her responsibility to escort him
through the arbor of the garden to the street, so
he could find his way home. This she promptly did.

And just as promptly,
Murray reappeared.

Twice more this was repeated.
Escorted out, Murray soon found
his way back to the garden. Escorted
out again, he came back again.
What could Madelyn do?
She opened her thermos to drink
some tea. Simple indeed; Murray
had arrived just in time for tea.

Later, some might say it
was love at first sight.
At the end of the day
Murray went home with her.
Yes, Murray had arrived
to stay. He moved into 1251,
settled into the house,
and joined Madelyn's business,
which soon became
"Gardening with Murray."

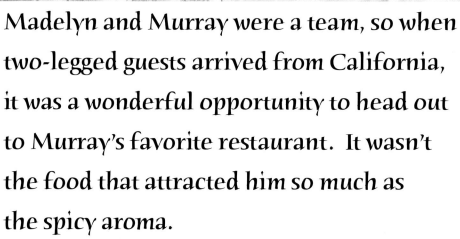

Madelyn and Murray were a team, so when two-legged guests arrived from California, it was a wonderful opportunity to head out to Murray's favorite restaurant. It wasn't the food that attracted him so much as the spicy aroma.

When they arrived at the restaurant the waiter showed Murray to his favorite corner resting place, where he could inhale the deep fragrances as the two-legged ones ate at the table.

When they were done they shared
a breezy drive through the brilliant
Seattle sunset. They made a quick
stop at the frozen yogurt shop,
then headed back to 1251. As the
two-legged ones went into the house,
Murray toddled up the steps to his
resting place on the front porch.
Two hours later he was gone.

Murray was not just in the wrong place. He usually liked to hang out on the cozy front porch as well as the comfortable living room. He was not in either place. This was not just a matter of a different location. No. Murray was gone.

GONE! No note, no message, no clue.
Just gone.

The two-legged ones were frantic, especially Madelyn the great lover of Corgis. Frantic. Not just concerned, not just worried, not just panicked ... but FRANTIC!

They searched everywhere. The two-legged ones spread out through the neighborhood, checking the alleyways, the streets, looking under the bushes, searching under the neighbors' houses ... no Murray. They walked for hours calling his name. No Murray.

All the two-legged ones but Madelyn collapsed from exhaustion and crawled into bed. Madelyn continued the search till the wee hours of the morning, under the dark Seattle sky. Murray was not to be found. Finally even Madelyn went to bed. Murray was gone. GONE!

After a fitful sleep, the two-legged ones awoke, ready to begin a new search. Again they hunted with no success.

And then, without so much as a "How do you do," without so much as a "Good morning," or even a "Top of the day to you, sir," Murray was back, tired and bedraggled, droopy-eyed, toddling up the steps to 1251.

The mystery of
where he had gone has
puzzled Murrayologists for years.
Researchers have come up empty.
Three Ph.D. candidates at the University
of Washington failed their orals because they could
not solve the puzzle. Last year's best seller "Murray's
Secret Life" was way off the mark. Last week's People
magazine article "Murray's Wild Night with J. Lo"
was a blatant grab for publicity. And the National
Enquirer headline "Murray Spotted with Elvis
in Spaceship" was, well, just a fabrication.

No, none of these stories could
answer the question ... where had Murray gone?

Where indeed?

Only now can the
story be revealed.
Remember that
Murray was a Corgi,
and no ordinary
Corgi at that.

For centuries there had been a feud among Corgis,
a feud between Cardigan Corgis and Pembroke Corgis.
The feud was bitter with broken friendships, lovers torn apart,
fortunes won and lost. It had gone on far too long, and on that
fateful night Murray had been summoned by the Queen.
Yes, the Queen ... Her Majesty ... the Queen herself ... the only
two-legged one who loved Corgis as much as Madelyn.

The Queen had summoned Murray to end this feud between Cardigan and Pembroke Corgis. The one Corgi with the wisdom to bridge the gap between the bitterly divided clans, because Murray was both a Cardigan Corgi and a Pembroke Corgi!

Ye Royal Summons

Murray,

So that night Murray had made his way
to I-5 South, stuck out his paw,
and headed for the airport.

Once he was safely aboard a Boeing 707, he made the flight to London, where the Queen humbly asked him for help.

She reminded Murray that before his explorations in the world had brought him to Madelyn, he was actually Montague, Sir Montague, the only Corgi she had ever knighted. She asked now that he grant her this favor, as the Queen was heartbroken by the sadness and hostility the feuding had brought to the world of the Corgis.

Murray started by meeting with individual
Corgis in small groups. He heard their
complaints and grievances, soothed those
who were angry, calmed those who were
upset. When one Pembroke Corgi
burst into tears, Murray
snuggled with her until
the tears were dry.

When one Cardigan Corgi howled in pain, Murray howled with him till the pain had been released.

Murray listened
carefully to those who had
problems to present, took the
problems seriously, and thought about solutions.
One very difficult issue had arisen among Pembroke and
Cardigan Corgis who were both assigned to the Queen's royal
procession. They agreed to share the leading role in the
procession, switching roles each month and alternating
holidays, a solution which brought smiles all around.

Finally, Murray met with the
ancestral leaders of the
Cardigan clan and the
Pembroke clan. Using his
patience, his kindness,
his insight, and his gentle
methods of persuasion,
he brought the leaders of the
warring clans to an agreement,
an understanding,
a final and complete end
to years of bitterness.

When all was completed, Corgis gathered by
the hundreds in traditional concentric circles.
Murray sat in the middle, leading the ancient
howling ritual. He set the tempo of the howl,
each Corgi joining in with his or her own style,
till thousands of Corgis were howling out
centuries of pain and frustration. Together they
howled in a new era of unity which bonded all
Corgis to each other in peace and harmony.

The next morning he caught the
early flight back to Sea-Tac Airport.

He hitched a
ride to Seattle
and made his
way up the
steps at 1251,
exhausted.

The two-legged ones were ecstatic, especially Madelyn.
Although Murray was glad to be home, all he could think
about was sleep. The two-legged ones were excited
to see him, but he was deeply content.

He had accomplished the greatest
achievement in the history of Corgis:
peace for all Corgis everywhere.
And now it was time to rest.

To the memory of my dear friend and partner, Eric Anthony Lowhar,
whose brilliant mind, numerous accomplishments, quest for knowledge and unique personality,
serve as an inspiration to all who knew and loved him.
March 2, 1950 - June 23, 2000.

And to Murray aka Mur-Mur &/or Doodles...A precious gift that came to me,
with whom I shared joy and happiness. An amazing being, I truely loved with all my heart.
.July 1987 - September 2, 2003.
— Madelyn Katzman

To Beth and Corie Lyn -
for their love and inspiration, despite horrible deadlines.
— Doug Keith

Murray's private night out; a semi-true story / by Matthew Rinaldi & Madelyn Katzman; illustrations by Doug Keith.
36-p. cm.

SUMMARY: Murray, a Corgi of noble lineage, mysteriously disappears from home when he is summoned by the queen
to end an age-old feud between the Pembroke (Welsh) and Cardigan Corgis.

Audience: Grade school to adult

ISBN 0-9761309-0-4

[1. Dogs—Fiction. 2. Conflict resolution—Fiction. 3. England—Fiction. 4. Seattle, Washington—Fiction]
I. Keith, Doug, ill. II. Title.
[Fic]

Library of Congress Control Number: 2004113974

Special Thanks:
Mad4Mur would like to thank the people that helped make this book possible: Matthew Rinaldi–author; Doug Keith–illustrator; Gail and Barb Wodzin–layout and design;
David Olivenbaum–editor; Colleen Morgan–research.

Book Layout and Design:
Rat Race Productions, Inc., Seattle

Printed in Canada

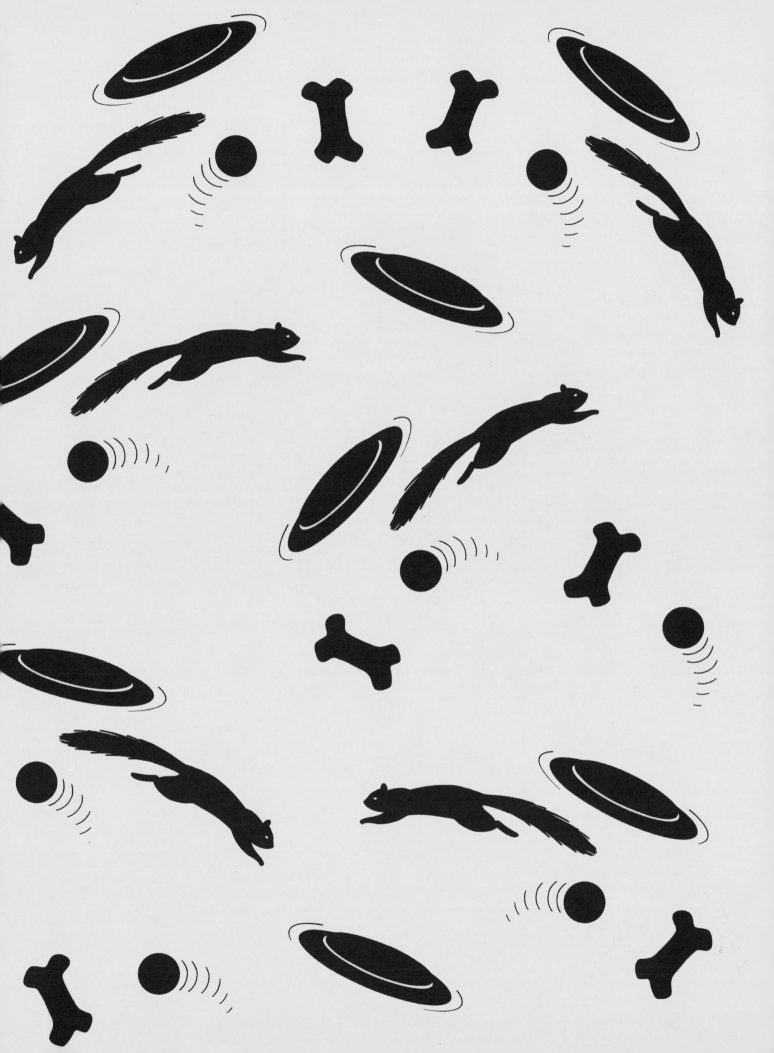